For Daisy and Rosie. Always follow your own path
and don't listen to boneheads! Love, Daddy xx

First U.S. edition 2014

Library of Congress Catalog Card Number 2013952830
ISBN 978-0-7636-7131-0

14 15 16 17 18 19 TLF 10 9 8 7 6 5 4 3 2 1

Printed in Dongguan, Guangdong, China

This book was typeset in Kosmik.
The illustrations were created digitally.

TEMPLAR BOOKS

an imprint of
Candlewick Press
99 Dover Street
Somerville, Massachusetts 02144
www.candlewick.com

GIGANTOSAURUS

Jonny Duddle

templar books
an imprint of Candlewick Press

Many million years ago,

beyond the path of the lava flow,

on the edge of the jungle, where the herbivores grazed,
four little dinosaurs spent their days
playing in the Cretaceous sun,
following tracks and having fun.

The dinosaur moms said,

Beware, my child . . .

of the GIGANTOSAURUS, so FIERCE and WILD!

With teeth as long
as you are tall,
he'd soon make a snack
of one so small.

His feet go STOMP!
His jaws go CRUNCH!
In the blink of an eye,
you'd be his LUNCH!

Bonehead, Tiny,
Fin, and Bill
went off to play
up on the hill.
The Gigantosaurus
was on their minds
till Bonehead said,

we need
a lookout,
and I'm the BEST!

I think
you'll find . . .

I'll get a
good view
from that
termite nest.

But it was only a minute before Bonehead cried,

It's the GIGANTOSAURUS!

Quick! RUN and HIDE!

THUD
THUD
THUD

They ran!
They hid!
They shook with fear!
The GIGANTOSAURUS
was coming near!

But there was no STOMP.
There was no CRUNCH.
No fierce monster
had smelled his lunch.

"It's just
TRICERATOPS!"
Bonehead declared.
"You ran! You hid!
You were all so
SCARED!"

Hello, Dad.

Hello, Son.

"But you passed
my emergency warning trial.
Now I'll keep watch
from that rock awhile."

But a little bit later, Bonehead cried,

The
GIGANTOSAURUS!
Quick—RUN and HIDE!

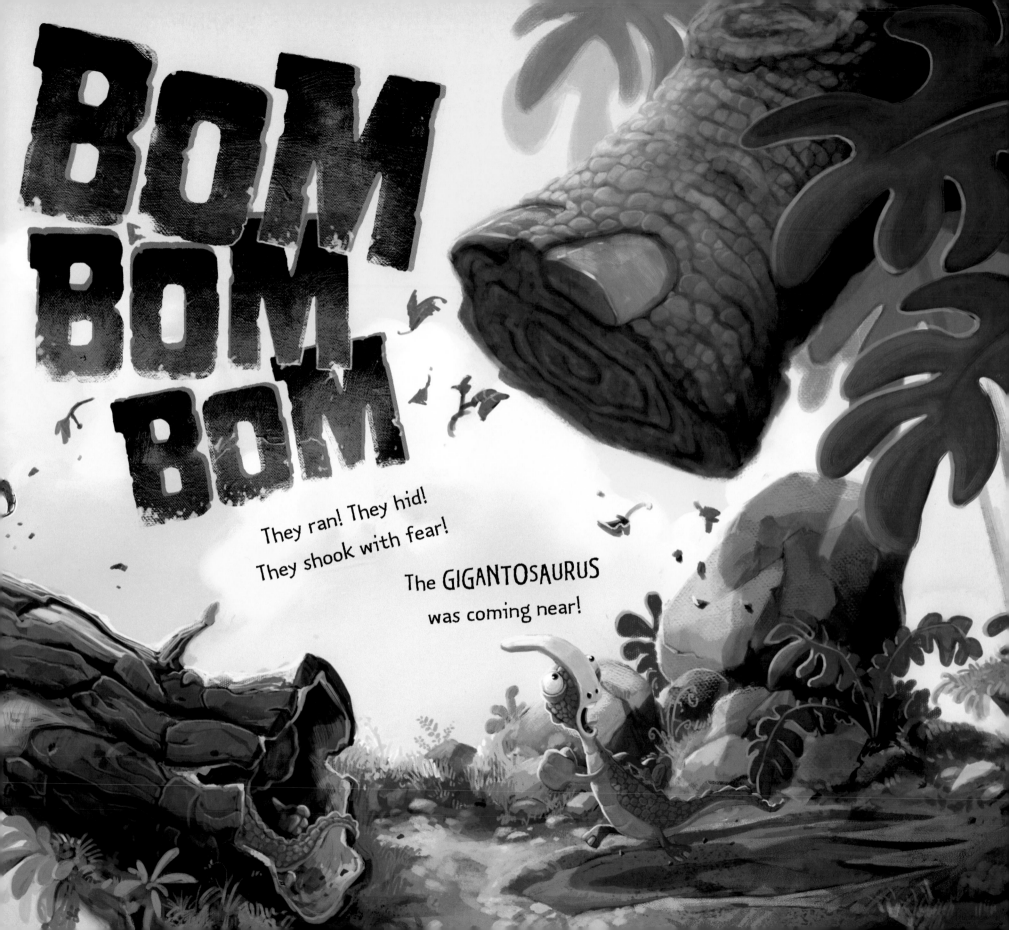

BOM
BOM
BOM

They ran! They hid!
They shook with fear!

The GIGANTOSAURUS
was coming near!

But there was no STOMP.
There was no CRUNCH.
No hungry beast after snacks to munch.

"It's old DIPLODOCUS!"
Bonehead declared.

"You ran! You hid!
You were all so scared!"

"But danger lurks,
as you need to learn.
I'll look out from that
enormous fern."

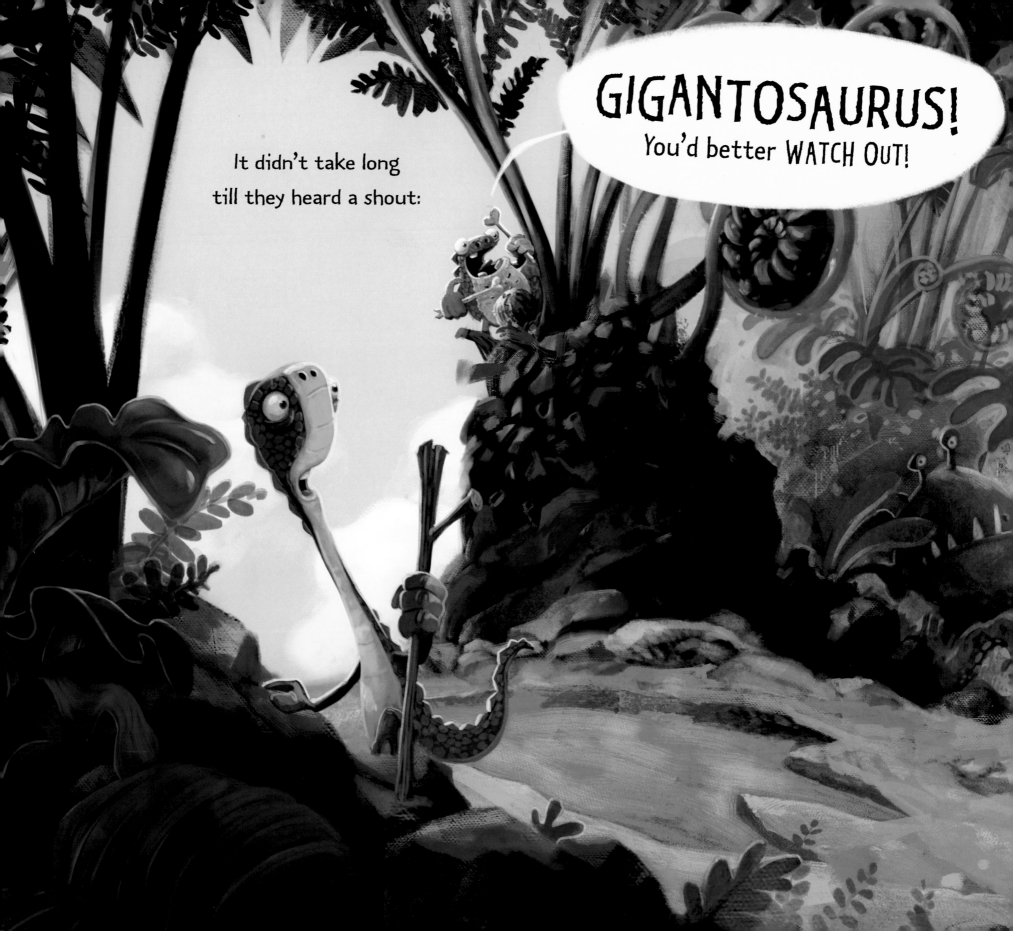

It didn't take long
till they heard a shout:

GIGANTOSAURUS!
You'd better WATCH OUT!

THUMP
THUMP
THUMP

They RAN! They HID!

They shook with fear!
The GIGANTOSAURUS

was coming near!

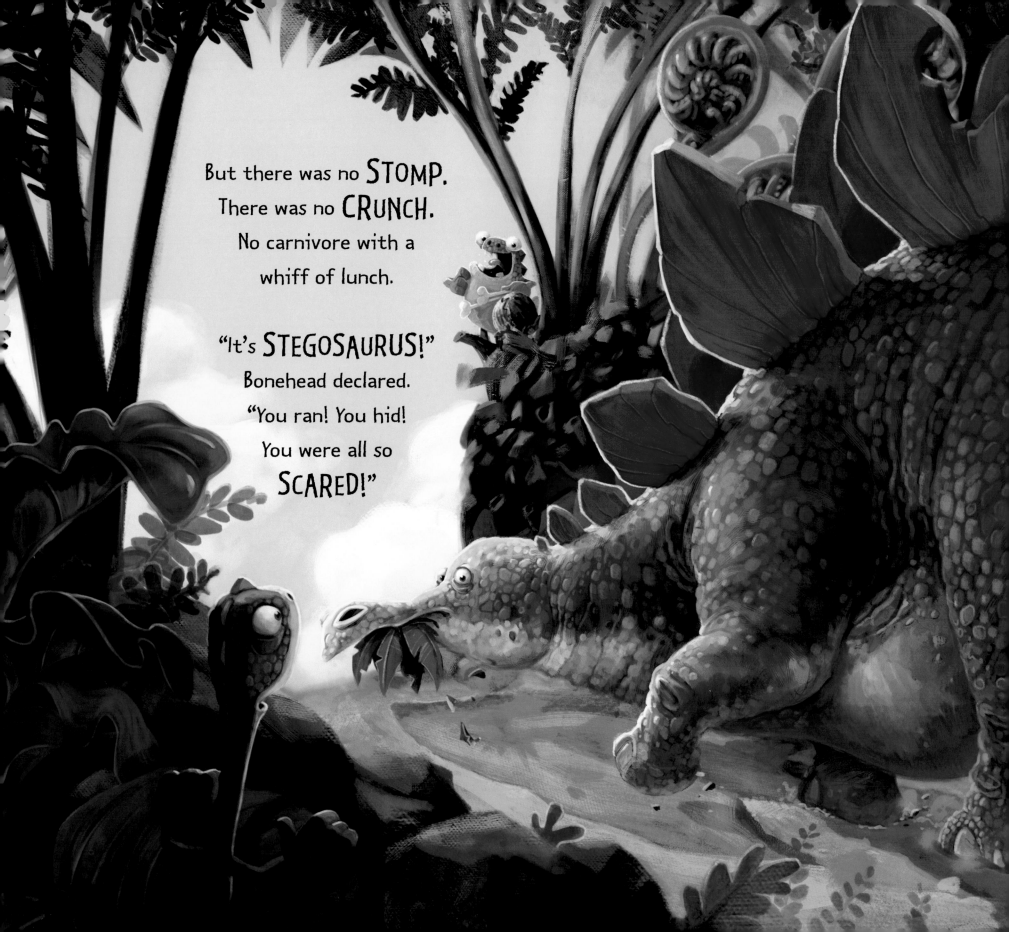

But there was no STOMP.
There was no CRUNCH.
No carnivore with a
whiff of lunch.

"It's STEGOSAURUS!"
Bonehead declared.
"You ran! You hid!
You were all so
SCARED!"

"But at least
you passed my final test.
Now I'll take a nap
in that comfy nest."

Then, seconds later,
the cry began:

GIGANTOSAURUS!
Run as fast as you can!

But although his friends heard
what Bonehead cried,
by now they knew
that Bonehead lied.

"That's it!" said Bill. "We're off to explore. And we're not going to play with YOU ANYMORE."

With everyone gone, Bonehead was alone.
He began to wish he was back home—
because an awful noise was coming near,
and now there WAS good reason for fear.
The feet went

STOMP!

The JAWS went **CRUNCH!**

And the GIGANTOSAURUS had his LUNCH!

Bonehead's friends came running back after they heard the tree go CRACK!

Poor old Bonehead— it's such a shame.

What a sad end to his naughty game.

BURP!

Even though he tricked and lied, at least he taught us how to hide.

But then they heard a muffled cry from the scraps of nest that lay nearby. . . .

I'm here!
It's ME! I survived!
I'm sorry that I tricked and lied.
But this time, honestly, it's true—
there's a PTERANODON
after you!

And though Bonehead thought they'd run in fright,
his friends just shrugged and said,
"Yeah, right!"

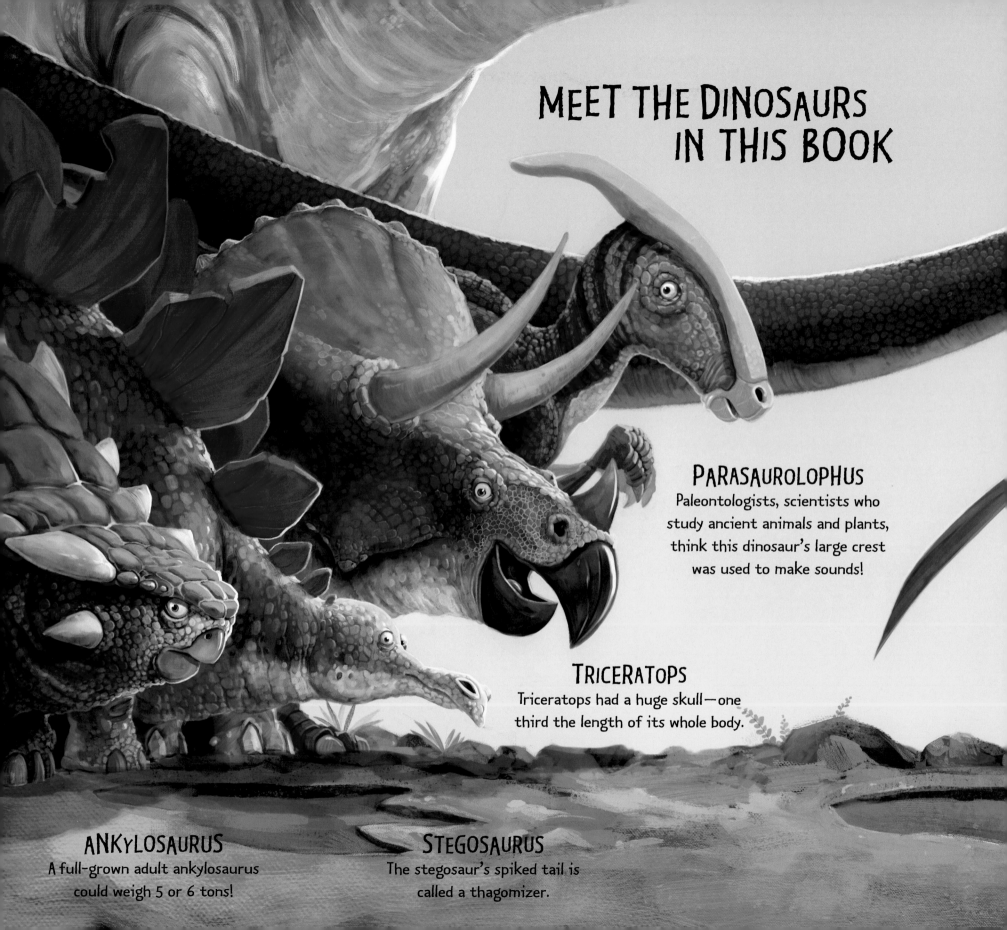

MEET THE DINOSAURS IN THIS BOOK

PARASAUROLOPHUS
Paleontologists, scientists who study ancient animals and plants, think this dinosaur's large crest was used to make sounds!

TRICERATOPS
Triceratops had a huge skull—one third the length of its whole body.

ANKYLOSAURUS
A full-grown adult ankylosaurus could weigh 5 or 6 tons!

STEGOSAURUS
The stegosaur's spiked tail is called a thagomizer.

BRACHIOSAURUS
Brachiosaurs were huge herbivores. Tiny's mom will grow to be even bigger than Diplodocus!

DIPLODOCUS
This giant dinosaur had a comically tiny brain.

PTERANODON
Pteranodons were flying reptiles. This one is a quetzalcoatlus, but Bonehead couldn't pronounce that.

GIGANTOSAURUS
This scary dinosaur was
made up for this book!*